ALAN C. JENKINS
THE GHOST ELEPHANT

an African story

Illustrated by Nelda Prins

Puffin Books

Puffin Books, Penguin Books Ltd, Harmondsworth, Middlesex, England
Viking Penguin Inc., 40 West 23rd Street, New York, New York 10010, U.S.A.
Penguin Books Australia Ltd, Ringwood, Victoria, Australia
Penguin Books Canada Limited, 2801 John Street, Markham, Ontario, Canada L3R 1B4
Penguin Books (N.Z.) Ltd, 182–190 Wairau Road, Auckland 10, New Zealand

———

First published 1981
Reprinted 1984, 1987

———

———

Made and printed in Great Britain by
Richard Clay Ltd, Bungay, Suffolk
Set in Monophoto Ehrhardt

PUFFIN BOOKS

THE GHOST ELEPHANT

In his imagination, Mimbe saw again the mighty elephant. He would be famous in the village when he brought news of it to the hunters. They would praise him and his name would go into one of their songs.

Soon the village had begun the hunt. Protected by the powerful magic of Karakiti, the village witch-doctor, they could not fail. It was a triumphant day. But then Karakiti refused the payment he was offered for his spells and the dreadful ghost of the mighty elephant returned in vengeance to terrorize the village. Or did it?

With the help of Messouf, the wily hare, Mimbe is left to unravel the mystery of the ghost elephant.

Alan C. Jenkins has for many years been active in natural history societies and has written many books on the subject, and has been published in several languages. He has contributed considerably also to the BBC Schools Broadcasting Department and nature magazines. He lives on Dartmoor and has studied wildlife extensively both in this country and abroad.

For Luke and Richard 2nd

CHAPTER ONE

Mimbe stared in wonder at the elephant. In all his ten years he had never before set eyes on such a huge creature. Surely there could not be another such giant in the whole of Africa. It must be the elephant of elephants, Samburu himself. At any moment the elephant might raise its trunk and shout out that he was king of the forest.

'I am Samburu, who makes the earth tremble!' he would trumpet.

'I am Samburu whose mighty tread causes the thunder!'

'I am Samburu whose fearful tusks gouge out the rivers and the lakes!'

For all this happened long ago in the days when men and animals could speak together. So Mimbe listened intently for any words that Samburu might utter.

He was so awestruck he almost forgot to be afraid. All the same, as he hid in the reeds at the edge of the river, he kept a watchful eye on the elephant. For it had finished bathing, finished squirting liquid mud over its grey wrinkled hide, and now, glistening in the slanting sun, was trudging off into the forest, while the snow-white egrets flew up in front of him.

Mimbe began to wriggle backwards. If Samburu got wind of him, he might be trampled to pulp. Mimbe shivered – and made the reeds rustle even more. A touraco cried out loudly. Kro! Kro! Kro! 'Get out! Get out! Quickly!' the bird was warning him. And in the branches of the acacia trees insects hissed and sizzled and clicked. Comfortably and coolly buried in the soil, a bull-frog croaked. Everybody seemed anxious for Mimbe, including Messouf the hare who went cantering past.

'Man!' he advised, his long ears flat on his back. 'You'd best get out of here, fast! Fast, man, fast!'

Mimbe heeded the warnings. He took to his heels and fled. Behind him he heard a violent crashing and splintering as the elephant put his great domed forehead against a tree and pushed it over – not to test his strength, but simply to get at the juicy leaves more easily.

Eager to tell his news to the men of the village, Mimbe ran swiftly homeward. His bare feet slapped the sun-baked earth. Grey parrots screeched at him, demanding the latest gossip. Monkeys swung in the branches and pretended they already knew. On through the tall tawny grass, past the swaying oil palm-trees, the boy ran.

Samburu! Samburu! he thought, his eyes bulging as he saw again in his imagination that mighty elephant. He would be famous in the village. He, Mimbe, would bring news of the great elephant to the hunters. They would praise him. His name would go into one of their songs.

'Samburu!' he yelled, his voice cracking shrilly. 'A huge elephant! The king of elephants! I, Mimbe, son of Gholo, have seen him! He makes thunder as he treads!'

That was not altogether true. You often could not hear the elephant as he walked along on his padded feet. In spite of his enormous size he could move quite silently when he wanted.

Mimbe had started to shout his tidings even before he came in sight of the blue smoke curling through the palm-thatched roofs. He passed women returning with bundles of firewood on their heads, others with clay pots from the well.

'Why are you in such haste, toto?' they teased him. 'Your mother has not cooked the fu-fu dumplings yet!'

'Make way, o chatterers!' he cried importantly, dodging past them. They made him cross, for he was far too old to be called 'toto'. 'The touraco bird does not croak as much – and is more brilliantly clad than you! I have news for the menfolk! News for the hunters! We go to hunt Samburu!'

'Ah, by my eye!' said one of the women, hopefully. 'May your words be true! There will be meat for all if the hunters' spears find their mark!'

The men of the village were squatting in front of the huts. They took snuff or smoked while waiting their turn to have their heads shaved by Tala the barber. They listened impatiently to the sound of women working; it was past suppertime and the men slapped their bellies as if to quiet the hunger within them. Or maybe in anticipation. Bongang the headman had a particularly handsome belly. It sounded like a drum when he slapped it.

'Samburu! A giant among elephants!' Mimbe's shrill voice burst in upon the lazy gossip. 'With my own eyes I saw him!'

'He has eaten green maize and dreamt this!' scoffed Tala, glancing up from his work and accidentally nicking his customer's scalp. 'Gholo! You should thrash your son for telling lies!'

'It is true!' shouted Mimbe, chest heaving. 'I nearly drowned in the wave he caused when he strode from the river!'

'Is it truly true, o Mimbe?' demanded Bongang, his eyes full of threat. 'What words did Samburu utter?'

'I did not stay to hear what he said,' admitted Mimbe, his own eyes rolling, for he did not want the men to think him a coward. 'I was all haste to bring the news to you. Besides, Samburu's mouth was stuffed with leaves and he did not speak clearly!'

'Is this true, my son?' asked Gholo. 'That you did indeed meet the elephant?'

'Ten thousand times true, my father!' Mimbe assured him. He darted down and clasped Gholo by the ankles. 'On my head I swear it! Ask Messouf the hare – he was there!'

Then the men of the village were convinced. Even supper was forgotten in their excitement. For once the women were amazed that the men had stopped grumbling that it was not ready. The fireflies flitted like silver jewels strung across the clearing. The monkeys jabbered fearfully as they settled for the night and hoped that no leopard would come near them. Yet still the men went on discussing Mimbe's news.

'Tomorrow we must hunt!' declared Bongang, taking an extra big pinch of snuff. 'Summon Kamwendo the great hunter that we may make our plans! But first,' he added hastily, 'we must consult Karakiti the witch-doctor. He must guard us against the might of Samburu! He must ward off the vengeance of the great elephant! No hunt can succeed without the magic skill of Karakiti!'

Nowadays witch-doctors have rather gone out of business. But at that time, Karakiti, the witch-doctor of Gwelo, flourished greatly. People went to him for advice on all matters, if the crops failed or the cattle suffered from the pest.

But especially when the men of Gwelo went hunting, they consulted Karakiti.

CHAPTER TWO

Karakiti the witch-doctor pranced and capered along the track. He bent over backwards till his body arched like a bow. He flung his arms wide as if to embrace the whole sky. His feathered head-dress flapped and rustled like the wings of the birds it had come from. His face was hideously streaked with white clay. His arms and ankles were strung with brass bangles that glinted in the sunlight. In his hand he brandished a cluster of bones that rattled with every movement.

And all the time the witch-doctor pranced along, he kept up a magic recital that nobody else could understand. But all the men who were following him knew that it was very powerful magic. They glanced fearfully at each other, their eyes wide, but they spoke not a word. It might have been dangerous to interrupt Karakiti's secret spells!

Silently, clutching their weapons, they followed the sorcerer through the head-high grass, confident that his magic would bring them successful hunting. Karakiti's fee would be high, but it would be worthwhile!

In single file behind the witch-doctor, the hunters padded on – Kamwendo the chief hunter – Bongang the headman – Gholo, Tembo, Mbea, Badoumdou, and all the others. And at the end of the procession Mimbe pattered, determined not to be left out of it all.

At first nobody had noticed his presence and afterwards it was too late to send him back. They had gone too far from the village by now. Besides, hadn't Mimbe brought the all-important news of the elephant? It was only fair that he should be allowed to join the hunt!

On the hunting party went, across the sun-scorched land that was as yellow as a lion. Far overhead the vultures were wheeling – they knew that when Kamwendo went hunting there would be rich pickings for them. But Kamwendo was beginning to scowl. He was well aware that it had been necessary to consult Karakiti and beg him to ensure success for the hunt and also to protect the men of Gwelo from evil spirits. All the same, he was thinking, how could they hunt successfully with all this din going on? Surely Karakiti had worked enough magic by now? At least the first part of it. And

Kamwendo muttered his displeasure to Bongang the head-man.

Karakiti heard the discontented mutterings going on behind him. Angrily he turned round and rattled the bones under Kamwendo's nose.

'Without my magic you will never succeed!' he cried, and his face was so hideous the men drew back in dismay, treading on each other's toes. 'Take care! I strive against many evil spirits for your sake! Without me you would be in dire peril!'

He turned again and proceeded on his way – and his head-dress was all at once snatched off by an overhanging branch of an acacia tree.

'See!' he shouted triumphantly. 'On all sides there are evil spirits waiting to pounce! Without me you would surely perish!'

He replaced his feathery head-gear and capered on again more wildly than ever – and promptly fell flat on his face in a cloud of red dust. Indeed, he almost disappeared from view and lay there with outspread limbs, his magic bones scattered all round.

'By my teeth!' exclaimed Bongang in alarm, peering through the dust. 'What magic does he perform now?'

Hurriedly the hunters dragged the witch-doctor to his feet. They dusted him down, retrieved his head-dress, which had fallen off again, and put the bones back in his hand. Karakiti had tripped over a hole made by a wart-hog in the den of an ant-bear. But of course everyone understood that it was not as simple as that.

'I wished to consult the earth-spirits,' Karakiti explained loftily. 'Certain of them dwell underground in the guise of a wart-hog. They advise me to protect you from behind. Otherwise evil spirits may creep up on you!'

So accordingly Karakiti went to the rear of the procession and Kamwendo was greatly relieved. Leaving the witch-doctor behind for the time being, he led the other men silently on. It was clear that by now they must be approaching the haunts of Samburu the elephant. Branches had been pulled down and snapped in pieces. Brilliant petals were strewn around. Whole trees had been pushed over and stripped of their leaves. It was as if a tropical storm had swept past. The elephant needed outsize meals for his out-size bulk and he just took food where he found it. After all, who could blame him? He had to live in the way he was made.

Now for the moment the witch-doctor's magic skill was forgotten. All that mattered was the hunter's skill. The men of Gwelo were intent only on Samburu's whereabouts. Carefully, tensely, as if they were stepping on prickly burrs, they crept on, eyes alert, ears alert, every sense alert. For they knew that the elephant might lurk in ambush for them and come charging out, trumpeting in anger.

'Take care!' the elephant would squeal. 'I am Samburu, king of the forest! I will crush you to pulp! You men will be like ants under my mighty feet!'

Suddenly Kamwendo came to a halt. He stooped down to examine the soil. Bongang and Gholo peered over his shoulder, breathing hard. Plain to see were immense round footprints, complete with four big toe-marks. Only a very big elephant could have made those tracks.

'Wah!' gasped Tala, rolling his eyes in dread. He was beginning to think that a barber's trade was safer than being a hunter. 'We are too small a band to tackle such a giant!'

'Silence!' Kamwendo hissed angrily. 'I will cut off your ears with a blunt knife if you make such a din!'

He glanced round slyly to see where Karakiti was. Then he stabbed his spear deeply into one of the elephant's footprints.

'That is my own magic!' he said in an undertone. 'Like that I can stop the elephant from escaping us!'

But the other men were uneasy, fearing that the witch-doctor would be offended at this.

Next, Kamwendo took up a pinch of dust from the ground and let it float from his fingers.

'Good!' he nodded. 'The wind is right. The elephant is on the other side of it. He will not catch our scent!'

Once again the hunters made their furtive way. Mimbe's heart was thumping so much he was afraid Kamwendo would scold him, too, for making a noise. Even the birds and the insects had grown silent as if they were listening.

Again the men came to a halt at a signal from their leader. A truly enormous pile of elephant dung lay before them. At once Kamwendo stuck his big toe in it, a real hunter's trick, that. It was the best way of knowing how long since the elephant had passed by. Kamwendo's eyes glinted. The blade of his spear winked as if reflecting them.

'Still warm!' the chief hunter whispered, in the voice of an expert. 'Samburu is not far away!'

At his orders the band of hunters spread out on either side through the tall grass. Inch by inch, clutching their spears, testing the strings of their bows, they advanced. Mimbe kept so close to his father that he almost tripped over Gholo's spear.

And all at once, there, ahead of them, through the acacia trees, appeared what at first seemed a vast grey cloud that filled the sky almost to the horizon. It was the imposing shape of Samburu the elephant.

Here was the tusked giant they had come to hunt.

Here was the mighty creature they had come to do battle with.

Brave deeds would be done; fearful dangers would be faced before they brought him low.

CHAPTER THREE

Samburu was dead.

The mighty elephant had been brought down.

Spears had thrust home. Arrows had flown straight to their mark.

The hunt had been triumphant.

But only because of Kamwendo's skill; only because of the bravery of men such as Gholo and Bongang and Mbea and Badoumdou! Without flinching they had faced their great foe!

At a respectful distance, weary but satisfied, the hunters sat regarding their huge victim. Ceaselessly they talked in whispers about the hunt. The more they whispered, the greater their daring deeds seemed to become. Each man's spear seemed to have been sharper than anyone else's. Each man's arrows had flown straighter. But on one fact they were all agreed: that the earth had trembled at the fall of Samburu!

And in the thorn trees the bald-headed vultures sat and listened to the whispering, hoping to join in the feast presently. And in the distance the jackals skulked and howled, begging the men to leave something for them. 'A few scraps for the poor!' they whined, and the hyenas uttered their ugly laugh: 'Bones! Bones! Any old bones?' they tittered.

The men did not like such talk; they guarded their prize jealously. All the people of Gwelo would feed well because of the successful hunt. For, just as the elephant himself had to live in the way he was made, so too did the people.

And sometimes, as now, the paths of elephant and men crossed – and one or other always had to give way.

But first now Karakiti the witch-doctor must perform the most important task of all. Respectfully the hunters – even Kamwendo – made way for him. It was possible that they could have hunted successfully without Karakiti's help. But though Kamwendo thought so, he admitted that they could not do without the witch-doctor's services now. What he was about to do would protect them from a far greater danger than the danger they had faced in hunting the elephant.

Grave-faced, the hunters watched as Karakiti, crouching, bowing, advanced towards the body of Samburu. Now his manner was very different. He no longer pranced and capered. He no longer uttered his shrill incantations. He did not even rattle his cluster of bones.

He bowed very low to the dead elephant, as if to a royal personage.

'O Father Elephant!' he exclaimed, in wheedling tones, his hands clasped in supplication. 'Listen to my humble words, I pray you! Hearken to Karakiti who addresses you on behalf of the men of Gwelo!'

'Ay,' murmured the hunters, squatting there; 'speak for us, o wise Karakiti!'

'O Father Elephant!' Karakiti continued, shuffling closer to the fallen giant, and bowing again – so low that his head-dress swept the dust. 'Great Captain! Majesty! It was not the men of Gwelo who slew you!'

'No, believe us, Lord, it was not us!' moaned the hunters – whose spears had thrust deep, whose arrows had darted so true!

'Great Captain! Great king of the forest!' Karakiti went on, while Samburu lay there grey and wrinkled and immense and forever still. 'It was not these men who killed you! They only happened to be passing by to gather wild honey! It was men from a village faraway – yonder   beyond the great river – beyond the rim of the earth. Great Captain, whose tread makes the thunder, it was other folk who brought you low! It was not our spears!'

'It was not our spears!' echoed the hunters, who but a few moments since had boasted of their skill in slaying Samburu the elephant – even though they had been careful to whisper it.

For they knew that all this was of the utmost importance. The elephant must not think that it was they who had killed it. Samburu must be persuaded that it was not they, the men of Gwelo, who had dared to hunt him, but somebody else. Never mind who – just anyone else as long as they themselves were not blamed!

Otherwise the ghost of Samburu the elephant would return to haunt them! Return and do them great harm!

In those ancient times brave hunters the world over feared this. They would face the sternest dangers during the hunt – stand unflinching before the charging foe – make light of their wounds – rescue their comrades from the jaws of death. But when they had slain their quarry they feared that its ghost would come back and haunt them. Even the Lapps in the far north were afraid that the spirit of a bear they had hunted would return and do them mortal harm. The Russians killed you! they would tell the bear. Not us! Not us!

All over the world the hunters of old tried to persuade their victims that somebody else had been to blame. For men believed that all the animals, the beasts and the birds and the serpents, possessed souls that could return to earth.

So it was now that Karakiti, the witch-doctor of Gwelo, spoke long and earnestly to the dead elephant, explaining that other men had brought about this calamity!

'Spare us a few bones!' the jackals continued to plead. 'Have pity on the poor, o valiant hunters!'

The hunters scowled and raised their fists. It was disrespectful of the jackals to shout out like that at such a solemn moment. Besides, if the spirit of Samburu heard them it might not believe the words of Karakiti.

'Great chieftain!' Karakiti begged hoarsely. 'We salute you, o mighty lord! Do not trample on us! Do not ruin our crops! It was not us who slew your majesty!'

Out in the lion-yellow grass Messouf the hare sat listening to all that went on.

'Man!' he said to himself, as he chewed thoughtfully on a leaf. 'If the springs always flowed as endlessly as the words of that old rogue Karakiti, there would never be a drought in all the land!'

CHAPTER FOUR

Now Karakiti the witch-doctor had carried out his important task. Now the villagers could live in peace, without fear of vengeance from the spirit of the elephant. Now they could enjoy a kingly feast of meat, washed down by beer, for the women had brewed especially for the feast (but they did keep some of the meat to dry for hungry days that might come). Now they could get on with their work, tending their crops or fishing in their canoes – or perhaps just sitting outside their huts as evening came on and taking a pinch of snuff to help their gossip along.

Karakiti had protected them from the ghost of Samburu.

Or so they hoped and believed.

But, needless to say, the witch-doctor had to be paid for his magic. Led by Bongang the headman, the men of Gwelo visited Karakiti in his thatched hut outside the village.

Badoumdou carried a stalk of bananas on his head.

Mbea brought a basket of yams.

Gholo brought some choice crayfish he had caught in the river. He knew all the best rocky places where the crayfish hid.

'Wonderful magician!' Bongang saluted. 'We have come to

reward you for the unearthly skill with which you have protected us from the ghost of Samburu!'

Karakiti was a long time replying. He took snuff from a cow-horn container and sniffed deeply, while his eyes glittered resentfully. For the witch-doctor had seen Kamwendo stab the elephant's footprint and he was jealous that anyone but him should dare to practise magic.

'You call this a fitting reward for my magic?' he complained at last. 'Am I a beggar that you bring me such trash?'

And scornfully he tipped over the basket of yams with his ivory-tipped staff.

The men of Gwelo were dismayed. In fact they were shocked by the witch-doctor's behaviour. They had thought the gifts were sufficient, even generous. For the villagers were not rich and this was all they could afford. But they were dismayed, too, because they knew it could be dangerous to offend the witch-doctor. They were simple people who felt he was far superior to them.

Uncomfortably the villagers huddled together, muttering in perplexity. They could not understand this. Why, what they had brought would feed a man – indeed, his family as well – for a whole moonful of days!

'We are poor!' Mbea grumbled to Bongang. 'It has been a harsh season. The rains fell thinly. We shall vie with the hyenas and search for carrion if this goes on. We cannot afford more.'

'We cannot afford to turn Karakiti against us!' Bongang said unhappily, his dark face gleaming as if it were polished. 'We need his protection against Samburu's ghost. Only the spells of Karakiti can ward off evil!'

So the men went away and fetched more gifts. Their womenfolk raised shrill voices in protest, saying there would

be nothing left for their own families to live on. But the men shrugged gloomily and returned to the witch-doctor's hut carrying golden cobs of maize, all that remained of last year's harvest.

'That?' Karakiti spat angrily, his pointed teeth glinting in the firelight. 'That is not enough for my pigs, if I had any! Beware, people of Gwelo! If you do not pay me as befits my skill, my spells may not work! Do not expect protection if you do not pay me my due!'

That night Mimbe could not sleep as he lay in his parents' hut. He listened to the lizards calling in the thatch. 'Tok! tok!' they were saying. 'Look out!' they meant. He listened to the fishing-owl hunting down by the river. 'Danger! danger!' he was sure it was saying. What if Karakiti caused his spell to fail out of spite? What if the ghost of the dead elephant should come and molest the village!

The ghost of Samburu!

Mimbe shivered as he lay staring at the needles of moonlight glinting through the chinks in the mud hut.

All at once Mimbe sat up, holding his breath. He listened keenly. Not to the fishing-owl or to the lizards. Nor to the snores of his family. But to something in the distance. A village dog had been howling at the moon or exchanging words with the jackals. But then the dog's howling changed to a sudden frantic barking and other dogs joined in.

A loud trumpeting rang out, almost splitting the night in two. A blundering hullabaloo was going on as if some monster was stamping and thrashing its way through the fields.

Gholo had woken up. In the dim light father and son stared wide-eyed at each other. Together they hurried out into the night. Other men stumbled out sleepily, too. Children were whimpering with fright.

'A storm is raging through the maize fields!' cried Mbea. 'We shall be ruined!'

'It is no storm! It is worse!' Bongang answered. 'We must go and see what is happening!'

'You go first,' the men said politely to Bongang. After all, he was the headman.

They lit torches and, holding the flaming brands high, made their way nervously towards the little fields. The gigantic din continued. The maize stalks rustled wildly. The shrill trumpeting rang out again.

And in the flickering light of the torches the men suddenly caught sight of an enormous figure rampaging through their crops. They could see the glinting tusks of an elephant. Its

mighty trunk snaked out and seized a sheaf of maize stems, thrust it into its mouth and then tore out another cluster by the roots.

All at once the elephant turned towards the men. Its eyes gleamed redly. Its huge tusks glinted menacingly. It raised its trunk and trumpeted again.

'Flee!' cried Bongang, and as he was headman of the village he always liked to set an example, so he was the first to flee. 'It is the ghost of Samburu! Flee for your lives! The spirit of the elephant has returned to take vengeance on us! Run for your lives!'

And the entire village fled from that fearful visitor! The women gathered up the totos in their arms, the grandmothers seized the older children by the hand, the dogs ran yelping at their heels, while in front of everybody ran the men. The people of Gwelo hid trembling in the forest while the elephant continued his fearful work. He trampled the crops, broke down many banana trees, ate up all the yams. Then he entered the deserted village and barged over some of the mud huts, stripped the thatch from the roofs and smashed up the canoes by the riverside.

'I warned you,' scowled Karakiti next day, when the frightened villagers crept back. He grinned up at them malevolently, his eyes narrow, his pointed teeth bared. 'You did not pay me proper respect. So my spells did not work. The ghost of Samburu has come back to make your lives miserable. You have only yourselves to blame!'

CHAPTER FIVE

In the grassy lands Mimbe was tending his father's goats. Leaning on his staff, he frowned deeply as he watched the animals browse. In the distance he could hear the men working as they repaired the damage caused by the ghost of Samburu. Gholo was re-thatching the roof of his hut. Mbea was mending his canoe. Badoumdou was clearing away palm-trees the ghost-elephant had uprooted.

Nobody sang. All Gwelo was downcast at what had happened – and terrified lest the ghost should come again. Some of the women had even suggested that they move to another place. But it was thought this would be useless – they would never escape the vengeance of Samburu's spirit.

Slashing at the grass, Mimbe slowly followed the bleating goats. All round him insects sizzled indignantly at being disturbed. Brilliant butterflies sailed past on gaudy wings.

Suddenly Mimbe came to a halt in mid-stride. Not far away a shrill cry had rung out. He guessed that something had been caught in a snare. One of Kamwendo's probably. The hunter had been trying to catch some wild piglings. But Mimbe knew it wasn't a pigling that was crying now.

He ran towards the sound and before long he caught sight of a tawny body heaving and vaulting, struggling and writhing in the grass, as it sought to escape from the snare. It was Messouf the hare and he had been caught by a hindleg. He was exceedingly cross and somewhat out of breath.

'Hey, man!' he asked sulkily, cautiously eyeing Mimbe's stick. 'Did you set this dratted snare?'

'It was not I!' Mimbe assured him. 'It's one of Kamwendo's. He was trying to catch a wild pigling.'

'Well, I'm no pigling, I suppose you can see!' Messouf retorted. His long ears drooped, his whiskers twitched irritably. 'Come on, then, man. Help me get out of it. Come on, man, do! Don't just stand there. You know folk don't eat me in these parts.'

That was true, Mimbe had to admit. People considered the hare a coward and that if they ate his flesh they might grow faint-hearted, too.

'By my long ears!' grunted Messouf presently, when Mimbe had released him. 'That's better! My leg was burning

so, it would have burst into flames if I'd been a moment longer in that snare. But, man, were you a time and a half showing up!'

That sounded a little ungrateful, to say the least, and Messouf must have realized this. For when he had flexed his leg and licked the sore place he sat up and said:

'Your folk in trouble, I hear, eh?'

This did not surprise Mimbe. The hare always knew the latest gossip. With his long ears he could not help hearing it.

'Man!' went on Messouf, sitting up and scratching. 'I passed by your village this morning and, man, it truly is in bad shape!'

'It was the ghost of Samburu,' muttered Mimbe, shaking his head dolefully. 'We failed to appease the spirit of the elephant after we had hunted him.'

'Who says so, man?' demanded Messouf, a blade of grass between his prominent front teeth. 'You can give me one guess. It was that old varmint who files his teeth – Karakiti? Am I right or am I wrong?'

Mimbe glanced admiringly at Messouf. The hare certainly never missed anything.

'We did not pay him enough,' said Mimbe. 'Besides, he was offended because Kamwendo tried some magic of his own. So Karakiti caused *his* magic to fail. Now we live in terror of Samburu's ghost!'

'Listen, man,' replied Messouf, with a kindly twitch of his whiskers. 'I don't usually reckon to meddle in folk's business. I reckon humans are quite able to take care of themselves, mostly. But you did me a good turn, so I intend to help *you*. Nobody can say Messouf doesn't pay his debts. Now, I'll tell you something, man. I don't believe one single word of that old witch-doctor of yours. It is my opinion that Karakiti is a fraud. What's more,' the hare added, chewing on the blade of grass, 'he's not a nice person to know. What does he file his teeth into points for, I would like to know?'

'But his magic, Messouf,' said Mimbe, anxiously. 'How can we find protection against the ghost of Samburu? We live in daily fear!'

'Firstly,' said Messouf, coolly, squinting watchfully at a hornet that went booming past, 'you can protect yourselves by helping yourselves instead of having any truck with the witch-doctor. Secondly, I don't reckon the elephant that smashed up your village is the ghost of Samburu, the one your hunters killed. And you can easily tell whether it is a ghost elephant or a real elephant.'

'How?' asked Mimbe, squatting down near the hare.

'Listen, man, and I'll tell you,' Messouf answered, sitting

38

up and scratching again. After he had scuffed vigorously at the back of his head, he continued. 'You go back to your village and tell Bongang all I've told you. He must summon the men of Gwelo, every man-jack of them. Boys as well. No shirkers, mind. He must get them to dig a great trench all round the village –'

'But it would have to be big – big as a ravine,' Mimbe protested. 'Beyond our power to dig.'

'Not so,' Messouf assured him. 'It's got to be wide, mind. Wide, let's say, as a tall man is tall. A bit more perhaps. You folk aren't all that tall.'

'All the same, it will mean a lot of work,' Mimbe shook his curly head doubtfully. He knew the men of Gwelo would not be very keen on that.

'Sure it will, man!' Messouf said sharply, grinding his teeth chidingly. 'But if you want to protect yourselves, you'll have to sweat for it!'

'Well, what then?' asked Mimbe, who could see the hare was right about that.

'I'll tell you, man,' the hare went on, a rather crazy glint in his eyes, Mimbe thought. 'The men of Gwelo have set to and built the trench, right? That's where I come in. I shall go and say a few words to that elephant. Between you and me, words he won't like. They'll get him in a real squealing mood. He'll chase me. Man, will he put his foot down –'

Messouf was so tickled at the prospect of what he had in mind that he fell over on his back, thumping his furry white belly in glee with his forepaws and kicking his long hind legs.

'He'll come pounding after me,' the hare continued when he had finished spluttering with laughter, 'and I shall lead him straight towards Gwelo –'

Mimbe sat up in alarm, the sunlight mirrored on his face.

'Man, you needn't worry,' Messouf promised. 'We'll soon see whether that elephant is a ghost or not. If that elephant can get across the trench without let or hindrance – no, what I should say, is, if he can get across that trench *at all*, then all right, he's a spirit, a ghost. But if he can't cross it, you'll know he's just a real, live, ordinary elephant.

'And that Karakiti is a cheat. And that you can do without the services of a witch-doctor!'

CHAPTER SIX

Day after day the men of Gwelo toiled. Day after day they dug at the red earth with their mattocks. Day after day the women carried away basketfuls of earth on their heads. The older children helped, too, and a never-ending line traipsed to and fro.

At first it had seemed a hopeless task. How could they ever dig a trench to keep out the elephant. And in any case, if that elephant was the ghost of Samburu as they feared, their labour would all be in vain.

When Mimbe hurried home with his startling news of what Messouf the hare had said, Bongang the headman at once summoned a meeting of the village elders. Gladly the men threw down their axes and cutty-knives and began to pass round a gourd of beer. But they grunted in dismay when they learned that even harder work faced them.

'Everyone knows that Messouf the hare is a little mad,' protested Badoumdou. 'It would be foolish if we took any

notice of what he says. There are times when he tries to jump
over the moon, he is so crazy.'

'We shall be in fearful peril if we heed the advice of
Messouf and ignore the warnings of Karakiti,' said Mbea.

'The ghost of Samburu will surely destroy us all,' added
Gholo, taking another swig of beer to give himself courage. 'It
would be best to pay the witch-doctor his fee and beg him to
strengthen his magic so that it protects us from this vengeful
spirit.'

'If we pay Karakiti what he demands,' Bongang pointed
out, snatching the gourd before Gholo could quite drain it,
'you will have to work far harder than merely digging a
trench!'

And little by little the headman persuaded the men of

Gwelo that it would be worthwhile giving Messouf's advice a try. He reminded them that the hare was said to have relations who were witches and that because of this he might well possess knowledge unknown to the villagers. Kamwendo supported Bongang, saying that he had often heard the hare grinding his teeth in a strange manner which Kamwendo was confident were secret messages. In addition, Messouf often thumped on the earth with his hind-feet and the hunter was certain the hare was communicating with his relations.

So the work had started. Every man in the village had filed out with mattock or mommetty on his shoulder. Every woman had come to help, for many were the loads of earth they would have to carry away.

The men worked with a will. They swung their digging-tools as one man and sang in chorus as they did so. The monkeys thronged the near-by trees to see what was going on. They chattered and grimaced among themselves, longing to find out and when they could not they simply told each other that the men had taken leave of their senses.

The men worked on steadily and their black skins shone like satin. The sweat ran from them and dripped on to their feet. Lurking not far away, Karakiti scowled darkly, for he did not like the sound of happy singing. Besides, like the monkeys he wanted to know what it was all about.

'You will anger the spirits!' the witch-doctor warned them, brandishing his bundle of bones. 'I am their messenger! Terrible things will happen if you ignore my advice! You will have only yourselves to blame if the ghost of Samburu returns! And next time he will trample Gwelo into the dust so that men will never know there was once a village here!'

Tala the barber trembled at all these threats but Bongang gave him a warning nudge. For the men had agreed that they would not tell the witch-doctor anything. So they took no notice of the rantings of Karakiti and sang more loudly than ever to keep up their courage.

Day after day the trench grew deeper. Day after day it encircled the village.

'Go and find Messouf,' Bongang ordered Mimbe, 'so that he can tell us whether we have toiled enough.'

'Man! That's a real trench!' exclaimed Messouf when he came lolloping to the village. 'By my long ears, if you always worked like that your storchouses would never be empty!'

'Is it deep enough?' Bongang asked anxiously. 'It is no deeper than Kamwendo is tall. And he is the tallest man in Gwelo! Is it wide enough? It doesn't seem all that wide to me! A man could leap across it!'

'Plenty wide enough, plenty deep enough!' Messouf chuckled, rubbing a paw over his muzzle and winking

45

knowingly at Mimbe. 'Right, man! I'll be off . . . to say a few words to that elephant!'

The villagers' eyes rolled nervously. The men of Gwelo were still somewhat fearful. They had yet to be convinced that Messouf's advice was sound. The women gathered up their totos on their backs and took them farther away to safety. The old people followed them. Tala the barber would have liked to go too, but he was ashamed.

CHAPTER SEVEN

Messouf the hare set off with a sprightly kick of his hind-legs. He flicked his ears from side to side, gave a jaunty twitch of his whiskers. Clearly he felt very important and was glad to have an audience, for Mimbe and several of the men followed him.

But they did so a little hesitantly, for the idea of purposely rousing Samburu's anger was full of danger, a ghost's anger was worse still. In fact, before long some of the men made excuses and turned back to the village.

'I have a thorn in my foot,' muttered Tala.

'I have not finished planting my maize,' mumbled Mbea.

But Gholo and Bongang and Kamwendo – and of course

Mimbe – continued after Messouf. They were all tingling with curiosity to see how Messouf would fare. Besides, most important of all, they were keen to see the hare's claim put to the test. If he could prove that the elephant was, as he said, just a real, live, ordinary elephant and not the spirit of Samburu, then their lives would be a great deal safer.

The men of Gwelo could cope with a real elephant, but a ghost elephant – wah! that was a different and desperate matter. What was more, they wanted to find out Messouf's secret knowledge. How could the hare tell?

Even Karakiti the witch-doctor followed, furiously hoping it would all end in disaster, but at the same time consumed with curiosity.

Messouf went straight off. At least, he did not go *straight*, for he kept leaping to this side and that, vaulting over a bush, jumping across a muddy pool. In fact, generally showing off.

But he knew very well where the elephant he was seeking was most likely to be at that hour of the day. He would be having his late afternoon bathe. Sure enough, before long Mimbe and the men could hear a huge splashing, a sound like a sudden cascade, a lashing of water as if the wind had got up.

Their steps became noticeably slower. Even Mimbe, for all his keen interest, began to creep cautiously through the undergrowth. But of course Messouf almost turned a double somersault in his glee. He knew his performance was about to begin.

'Watch this, man!' he said grandly and lolloped down to the water's edge. Not far out in the river stood the elephant, massive, majestic, resting his tusks on the branch of a near-by tree to ease the weight on his neck. Around him the egrets stood hunched on one leg, making up their minds to go off to roost. A pair of jackals had stolen down to drink and immediately started to whine for alms when they caught sight of the men. Messouf greeted them cheerfully: the bigger the audience, the better pleased he was.

'Man! Only a dirty person would need to bathe so much,' he declared to the world at large. 'Look at him out there! No wonder the water is always foul, with old big ears stirring it up!'

The elephant picked up a stick in its trunk and reached round to scratch its back with it and this set Messouf off again.

'Man! Only someone covered in ticks would need to scratch himself like that!' he exclaimed.

The men shifted uncomfortably in their hiding-places. It was truly alarming to hear the mighty Samburu being so insulted. Even the egrets had taken off, not liking to hear such rudeness. At first, however, the elephant seemed unaware of Messouf's impertinence, but Mimbe saw his eyes glint redly in the evening light. Mimbe hoped they had not been unwise to heed Messouf's boast. That elephant certainly looked fearful enough to be the ghost of Samburu.

The ghost of Samburu! The ferns rustled as the men trembled at the thought!

'Man!' Messouf chattered on. 'Just look at him! You'd think he was a travelling-merchant from some great city with his baggy trousers falling down! That's just what he looks like!'

And Messouf threw himself on his back, laughing so loudly that the jackals scuttled off with an uneasy glance at each other. As for the men, they too began to disappear. They were certain Samburu would not stand much more of the hare's impudence. Indeed, the elephant had started to wade slowly out of the river. You didn't really see him moving, he just seemed to float nearer the shore.

'Man! Look at that nose!' Messouf observed, with a wave of his paw. 'Shall I tell you how he got that ridiculous trunk? It's a rather shameful story –'

The men of Gwelo never heard the rest. For Samburu really had had enough. While the water lapped stormily on the shore, he strode out of the river.

'Man! That's done it!' sniggered Messouf, with great satisfaction. But no one stayed to listen. The villagers had already fled and they ran faster still when they heard the elephant crashing on his furious way. Mighty, awe-inspiring, trumpeting with rage, the elephant strode ever faster, brushing aside the branches as if they were twigs.

Even Messouf put on his best speed to begin with. But after a while he sat coolly in the path of the oncoming elephant, scratched himself, and then turned and cantered on again before the raging giant caught up.

'We shall pay dearly for this if Messouf has lied!' gasped Bongang, his face grey with terror. 'The elephant is so angry he can surely only be the spirit of Samburu! Ah, why did we ever listen to that fool of a hare! We are doomed! The ghost-elephant will trample us to pulp!'

'Man! This is only the start of it, I'm telling you!' Messouf shouted encouragingly to him.

But for the people of Gwelo it did not seem that it was the beginning. They felt rather that it must be the end – the end for all of them, in face of Samburu's fury. They bitterly regretted having listened to Messouf. There was now no doubt in their minds that this was the ghost of Samburu who would now take unspeakable vengeance on them for hunting him.

If only they had paid Karakiti's fee and made certain that his spell worked! Instead, they had listened to the prattlings of that long-eared chatterer!

As for Karakiti the witch-doctor, though he was filled with glee because things were going wrong, he skedaddled as quickly as anyone to escape from the charging Samburu.

CHAPTER EIGHT

Swiftly the men fled towards the village. But far more swiftly came Samburu the vengeful spirit. He did not run, but came on in rapid strides, fast as a horse could have galloped, while the red dust spurted out in thick clouds behind him.

In the village of thatched mud-huts the women scuttled this way and that, the children with them. Their voices rose in a shrill hullabaloo, for they did not know what to do as they watched their frightened menfolk running home. And now the trench had to be crossed! The trench that was supposed to protect them!

At full tilt Kamwendo took a flying leap and landed on the other side. Gholo followed him. Karakiti tried to jump but did not succeed. He clung on to the far side by his finger-tips and then went sprawling into the trench, screeching at the men to help him, but nobody could spare a thought for the witch-doctor at such a moment.

As for Mimbe, he knew he could not jump that trench. So he darted off out of the way into the thorn bushes, knowing he was safe for the time being, as Samburu was intent only on catching up with Messouf.

Samburu, trumpeting his rage, had only one thought – to trample that insolent hare into the dust until nothing but his shape remained stamped forever on the earth!

In terror the people watched as Samburu drew closer, a whirlwind of wrath. They were not concerned for the fate of Messouf, he could look after himself. They were simply horror-stricken at the thought of that all-powerful ghost-elephant coming closer and closer, his trunk raised in squeal after angry squeal, his ears standing out like sails.

If the people had been able to leap across the trench, how could it ever be enough to stop Samburu?

Now Messouf himself put on a burst of speed. Straight towards the village he ran. Then, when he was a few feet from the edge of the trench, he took off in an agile, curving leap. It was clearly a special effort and Messouf even performed a little jinking wiggle in mid-air, for he knew that all eyes were on him. With ease and grace he vaulted clean across the trench and landed on the other side – where, to the extreme astonishment of the villagers, he sat down calmly and began to scratch as if nothing untoward had gone on.

'Man!' he complained. 'We could do with a shower of rain to lay this dust. How it does get into one's fur!'

And nearer, ever nearer came the furious Samburu, watched by the villagers whose limbs turned to stone, so motionless did they stand and stare. It was then, in that blood-chilling moment when the people of Gwelo thought their last hour had come that a strange thing happened; an exceedingly strange thing.

All at once Samburu caught sight of the trench. His trumpeting ceased abruptly. His ears no longer spread in anger. He dug in his huge feet and began to skid through the churning dust. He even lowered his immense hindquarters to stop his onward rush.

In a billowing red smoke of dust he came to a violent halt at the very brink of the trench.

'Wah!' said the men of Gwelo as one man. They looked disbelievingly from one to another, while, unheard, Karakiti continued to screech down there in the trench.

Yet all this time Messouf the hare nonchalantly sat there, scratching as if he was unaware of what had happened. As for the elephant, he stood there dimly huge in the red dust that floated around him. Then, while the astonished people watched, he turned slowly away and began to trudge back towards the forest, head bowed, ears drooping, trunk dangling.

'Well, man!' said Messouf airily, to nobody in particular.

56

'What did I tell you? There's your proof! That's no spirit you see before you. That's an ordinary, plain, real, live elephant. And right now he's feeling a tiny bit smaller than he would like. Haw! Haw! Haw!'

Nobody spoke. Nobody knew what to say. Everyone was too dumb-founded by what they had seen. Messouf was rather irritated that the people were silent instead of praising him. The only person who had anything to say was Karakiti, who was spluttering with dust.

'Want to see it done again, man?' demanded Messouf. He ran at the trench, made another spectacular leap across it and cantered after the retreating Samburu. 'Hey, man!' he called out. 'What you go home for so soon? That's bad manners, not staying for supper when these folk had invited you along! Plantains – yams – maize – help yourself! You trying to slim, man?'

For a while the elephant took no notice of these gibes. But it happened that as he trudged on, he brushed against a wild bees' nest. Though his wrinkled, dust-coated hide was thick enough to resist them, if there was one thing the elephant detested it was bees buzzing anywhere round his trunk. And in his angry mood he blamed everything on that hare.

He wheeled about and once again strode wrathfully after Messouf. This of course was exactly what Messouf wanted. Lolloping, cantering, putting on a burst of speed whenever necessary, Messouf led the elephant back towards the village and, forgetting what had gone before, the elephant pursued him.

And once again the villagers watched in dismay, wondering why that stupid Messouf could not have left well alone.

And some of the men who had been in the act of dragging Karakiti out of the trench, immediately let him go again and

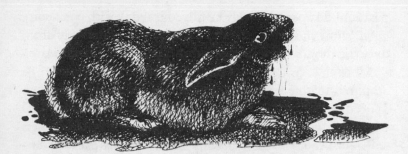

he sprawled on his back once more, shouting vainly for help.

Once again Messouf made his spectacular leap across the trench. Once again Samburu was forced to dig in his feet and skid to a halt. It was all perfectly true, what Messouf the hare had said. That elephant was no spirit, no ghost. Not by any manner of means could Samburu cross the trench. He was, as Messouf had all along claimed, just a real, live, ordinary elephant.

'You see, folk,' explained Messouf, for by now all the villagers were crowding round him, convinced beyond doubt of what he had promised them. 'It's like this. The elephant – he's big – mighty – strong – king of the forest and all that! But he can't jump! He just can't jump! A great big fellow like that and he can't jump! Fancy that now! But some of us can jump, eh, man? Watch this!'

And Messouf the hare was so pleased with himself he took another splendid leap across the trench. The dejected elephant was already on his way back to the forest, but the words of the boastful Messouf vexed him unbearably. He knew it was useless charging back again, for he would only be defeated by the trench. But he was at that moment plodding past a muddy pool. Quickly he filled his trunk with poto-poto, good, slimy mud, then turned and squirted it all, every drop, over the unwary Messouf, who leapt out of the way too late.

Messouf's pride was considerably hurt, for it has to be admitted that he was now far less spick and span than usual. Indeed, with all that mud sticking to his glossy fur he looked extremely bedraggled, but the onlookers politely hid their sniggers. And Messouf speedily recovered his usual jaunti-ness and laid on a special display of jumping. He was still showing off his skill, leaping time after time across the trench, when the fireflies started to flicker to and fro again and the tropical night came swiftly down like a velvet curtain.

'Man! Am I good and am I good!' panted the hare. 'Am I the greatest!'

And the villagers duly applauded him, for they were deeply grateful for what he had done. He had proved beyond doubt that the elephant was not the terrifying spirit Karakiti had

made them believe, the ghost of the animal they had hunted. For it is an extraordinary fact that no elephant can jump: no, that mighty, majestic animal just cannot jump and cannot even stride more than a couple of yards or so. No wonder that elephant had been so put out when he suddenly found himself faced by the trench. That trench was a fine protection and the Gwelo folk realized that all their sweat and toil had been worthwhile.

What is more, Messouf the hare had done something else for them. He had made it quite clear that Karakiti was a fraud. The witch-doctor had been completely discredited and in future he had to work for a living like everyone else, instead of taking advantage of people's fears and superstitions.